Clifford's
PALS

Story and pictures by NORMAN BRIDWELL

SCHOLASTIC INC.

New York Toronto London Auckland Sydney
Mexico City New Delhi Hong Kong Buenos Aires

For Ben Liyanage

ISBN-13: 978-0-590-44295-4
ISBN-10: 0-590-44295-3

62 61 60 59 58 57   10 11 12 13 14/0

Printed in the U.S.A.   40

Hello. This is my dog, Clifford.
I ride him to school every schoolday.

Clifford usually waits for me in the school yard.
One day he got tired of hanging around...

...so he went off to play with his pals.

The other dogs were Susie, Lenny, Basker...

...Flip, and a big dog named Nero. Nero led them.

He led them to a construction site. There were
a lot of men and machines there. Clifford
knew it was a dangerous place to play, but he didn't
want to look like a coward.

Some workers were knocking down old walls
with a big steel ball. Clifford thought the
ball would be fun to play with.

The men didn't think it was fun.
Clifford and his pals ran off fast.

Just as Flip was running under a scaffold,
a can of red paint spilled. The painter
yelled, "Watch out, little dog!"

Clifford peeked around the corner.

"*Little* dog!?" the painter said.

"What was in that paint anyhow?"

Susie, Lenny, and Nero jumped down into a big pit. The work crew didn't see the dogs. They started to pour cement on them.

Clifford knocked the cement chute aside.

Now the men were covered with wet, sticky cement.
Clifford cleaned them off.
Yuck! The cement tasted awful.
Clifford went to get a drink from a hose.

Just then someone turned the water on full blast.

Oh, oh.

Then Clifford saw the other dogs digging in some soft dirt. They didn't see that the bulldozer was about to push more dirt down on them.

Clifford jumped to stop the bulldozer.

He stopped it.

Next Clifford's pals found some great big pipes
to play in. Clifford tried to follow them.

But he was too big.

The pipe was stuck on Clifford's nose
and he couldn't see. Oooops.

The pipe came off.

The workers were angry. The dogs were
causing a lot of trouble for them.
They chased Clifford's pals into a storage pen
and locked them in.

Clifford came to rescue his pals.
He had already broken a crane, a bulldozer,
and a pipe. He didn't want to do any more
damage. So instead of breaking down the
fence...

...he found another way to help his friends.

Now the workers were even more angry. They tossed
a big strong net over Clifford and tied him.

They said they would have to keep him there until
the job was done. Clifford didn't know what to do.

But his pals did. They chewed through the ropes that
held Clifford.

They all ran back to the school yard.
Clifford and his pals decided they would never
play near a construction site again.